'The lower jaw was thin-what can I call it?-shallow, like a beast's; teeth showed behind the black lips…'

M. R. JAMES
Born 1 August 1862, Goodnestone, United Kingdom
Died 12 June 1936, Eton, United Kingdom

'Canon Alberic's Scrap-Book' and 'The Mezzotint' first
collected in *Ghost Stories of an Antiquary*, 1904; 'The Rose
Garden' and 'The Stalls of Barchester Cathedral' first
collected in *More Ghost Stories*, 1911.

ALSO PUBLISHED BY PENGUIN BOOKS
Count Magnus and Other Ghost Stories · *The Haunted Dolls'
House and Other Ghost Stories*

M. R. JAMES

Canon Alberic's Scrap-Book

PENGUIN BOOKS

PENGUIN CLASSICS

Published by the Penguin Group
Penguin Books Ltd, 80 Strand, London WC2R ORL, England
Penguin Group (USA) Inc., 375 Hudson Street, New York, New York 10014, USA
Penguin Group (Canada), 90 Eglinton Avenue East, Suite 700, Toronto, Ontario,
Canada M4P 2Y3 (a division of Pearson Penguin Canada Inc.)
Penguin Ireland, 25 St Stephen's Green, Dublin 2, Ireland (a division of Penguin Books Ltd)
Penguin Group (Australia), 250 Camberwell Road, Camberwell, Victoria 3124, Australia
(a division of Pearson Australia Group Pty Ltd)
Penguin Books India Pvt Ltd, 11 Community Centre, Panchsheel Park,
New Delhi – 110 017, India
Penguin Group (NZ), 67 Apollo Drive, Rosedale, North Shore 0632, New Zealand
(a division of Pearson New Zealand Ltd)
Penguin Books (South Africa) (Pty) Ltd, 24 Sturdee Avenue, Rosebank, Johannesburg 2196,
South Africa

Penguin Books Ltd, Registered Offices: 80 Strand, London WC2R ORL, England

www.penguin.com

Selected from *Count Magnus and Other Ghost Stories*, published in Penguin Classics 2005
This edition published in Penguin Classics 2011

3

Typeset by Jouve (UK), Milton Keynes
Printed in England by Clays Ltd, St Ives plc

ISBN: 978-0-141-19601-5

www.greenpenguin.co.uk

Penguin Books is committed to a sustainable future
for our business, our readers and our planet.
The book in your hands is made from paper
certified by the Forest Stewardship Council.

Contents

Canon Alberic's Scrap-Book

St Bertrand de Comminges is a decayed town on the spurs of the Pyrenees, not very far from Toulouse, and still nearer to Bagnères-de-Luchon. It was the site of a bishopric until the Revolution, and has a cathedral which is visited by a certain number of tourists. In the spring of 1883 an Englishman arrived at this old-world place – I can hardly dignify it with the name of city, for there are not a thousand inhabitants. He was a Cambridge man, who had come specially from Toulouse to see St Bertrand's Church, and had left two friends, who were less keen archaeologists than himself, in their hotel at Toulouse, under promise to join him on the following morning. Half an hour at the church would satisfy *them*, and all three could then pursue their journey in the direction of Auch. But our Englishman had come early on the day in question, and proposed to himself to fill a notebook and to use several dozens of plates in the process of describing and photographing every corner of the wonderful church that dominates the little hill of Comminges. In order to carry out this design satisfactorily, it was necessary to monopolize the verger of the church for the day. The verger or sacristan (I prefer the latter appellation, inaccurate as it may be) was accordingly sent for by the somewhat brusque lady who keeps the inn of the Chapeau Rouge; and when he came, the Englishman found him an unexpectedly interesting object of study. It was not in the personal appearance of the little, dry, wizened old man that the interest lay, for he was precisely like dozens of other church-guardians in France, but in a curious furtive, or rather hunted and oppressed, air which he had. He was perpetually half glancing behind him; the muscles of his back and shoulders seemed to be hunched in a continual nervous contraction, as if he were expecting every moment to find himself in the clutch of an enemy. The Englishman hardly knew whether to put him down as a man haunted by a fixed delusion, or as one oppressed by a guilty conscience, or as an unbearably henpecked husband. The probabilities, when reckoned up, certainly pointed to the last idea; but, still, the impression conveyed was that of a more formidable persecutor even than a termagant wife.

However, the Englishman (let us call him Dennistoun) was soon too deep in his notebook and too busy with his camera to give more than an occasional glance to the sacristan. Whenever he did look at him, he found him at no great distance, either huddling himself back against the wall or crouching in one of the gorgeous stalls. Dennistoun became rather fidgety after a time. Mingled suspicions that he was keeping the old man from his *déjeuner*, that he was regarded as likely to make away with St Bertrand's ivory crozier, or with the dusty stuffed crocodile that hangs over the font, began to torment him.

'Won't you go home?' he said at last; 'I'm quite well able to finish my notes alone; you can lock me in if you like. I shall want at least two hours more here, and it must be cold for you, isn't it?'

'Good Heavens!' said the little man, whom the suggestion seemed to throw into a state of unaccountable terror, 'such a thing cannot be thought of for a moment. Leave monsieur alone in the church? No, no; two hours, three hours, all will be the same to me. I have breakfasted, I am not at all cold, with many thanks to monsieur.'

'Very well, my little man,' quoth Dennistoun to himself: 'you have been warned, and you must take the consequences.'

Before the expiration of the two hours, the stalls, the enormous dilapidated organ, the choir-screen of Bishop

John de Mauléon, the remnants of glass and tapestry, and the objects in the treasure-chamber, had been well and truly examined; the sacristan still keeping at Dennistoun's heels, and every now and then whipping round as if he had been stung, when one or other of the strange noises that trouble a large empty building fell on his ear. Curious noises they were sometimes.

'Once,' Dennistoun said to me, 'I could have sworn I heard a thin metallic voice laughing high up in the tower. I darted an inquiring glance at my sacristan. He was white to the lips. "It is he – that is – it is no one; the door is locked," was all he said, and we looked at each other for a full minute.'

Another little incident puzzled Dennistoun a good deal. He was examining a large dark picture that hangs behind the altar, one of a series illustrating the miracles of St Bertrand. The composition of the picture is well-nigh indecipherable, but there is a Latin legend below, which runs thus:

Qualiter S. Bertrandus liberavit hominem quem diabo-
lus diu volebat strangulare. [How St Bertránd delivered
a man whom the Devil long sought to strangle.]

Dennistoun was turning to the sacristan with a smile and a jocular remark of some sort on his lips, but he was confounded to see the old man on his knees, gazing at the picture with the eye of a suppliant in agony, his hands tightly clasped, and a rain of tears on his cheeks. Dennistoun naturally pretended to have noticed nothing, but the question would not away from him, 'Why should a daub of this kind affect anyone so strongly?' He seemed to himself to be getting some sort of clue to the reason of the strange look that had been puzzling him all the day: the man must be a monomaniac; but what was his monomania?

It was nearly five o'clock; the short day was drawing in, and the church began to fill with shadows, while the curious noises – the muffled footfalls and distant talking voices that had been perceptible all day – seemed, no doubt because of the fading light and the consequently quickened sense of hearing, to become more frequent and insistent.

The sacristan began for the first time to show signs of hurry and impatience. He heaved a sigh of relief when camera and notebook were finally packed up and stowed away, and hurriedly beckoned Dennistoun to the western door of the church, under the tower. It was time to ring the Angelus. A few pulls at the reluctant rope, and the great bell Bertrande, high in the tower, began to speak, and swung her voice up among the pines and down to the valleys, loud with mountain-streams, calling the dwellers on those lonely hills to remember and repeat the salutation of the angel to her whom he called Blessed among women. With that a profound quiet seemed to fall for the first time that day upon the little town, and Dennistoun and the sacristan went out of the church.

On the doorstep they fell into conversation.

'Monsieur seemed to interest himself in the old choir-books in the sacristy.'

'Undoubtedly. I was going to ask you if there were a library in the town.'

'No, monsieur; perhaps there used to be one belonging to the Chapter, but it is now such a small place –' Here came a strange pause of irresolution, as it seemed; then, with a sort of plunge, he went on: 'But if monsieur is *amateur des vieux livres*, I have at home something that might interest him. It is not a hundred yards.'

At once all Dennistoun's cherished dreams of finding priceless manuscripts in untrodden corners of France flashed up, to die down again the next moment. It was probably a stupid missal of Plantin's printing, about 1580. Where was the likelihood that a place so near Toulouse would not have been ransacked long ago by collectors? However, it would be foolish not to go; he would reproach himself for ever after if he refused. So they set off. On the way the curious irresolution and sudden determination of the sacristan recurred to Dennistoun, and he wondered in a shamefaced way whether he was being decoyed into some purlieu to be made away with as a supposed rich Englishman. He contrived, therefore, to begin talking with his guide, and to drag in, in a rather clumsy fashion, the fact that he expected two friends to join him early the next morning. To his surprise, the announcement seemed to relieve the sacristan at once of some of the anxiety that oppressed him.

'That is well,' he said quite brightly – 'that is very well. Monsieur will travel in company with his friends; they will be always near him. It is a good thing to travel thus in company – sometimes.'

The last word appeared to be added as an afterthought, and to bring with it a relapse into gloom for the poor little man.

They were soon at the house, which was one rather larger than its neighbours, stone-built, with a shield carved over the door, the shield of Alberic de Mauléon, a collateral descendant, Dennistoun tells me, of Bishop John de Mauléon. This Alberic was a Canon of Comminges from 1680 to 1701. The upper windows of the mansion were boarded up, and the whole place bore, as does the rest of Comminges, the aspect of decaying age.

Arrived on his doorstep, the sacristan paused a moment.

'Perhaps,' he said, 'perhaps, after all, monsieur has not the time?'

'Not at all – lots of time – nothing to do till tomorrow. Let us see what it is you have got.'

The door was opened at this point, and a face looked out, a face far younger than the sacristan's, but bearing something of the same distressing look: only here it seemed to be the mark, not so much of fear for personal safety as of acute anxiety on behalf of another. Plainly, the owner of the face was the sacristan's daughter; and, but for the expression I have described, she was a handsome girl enough. She brightened up considerably on seeing her father accompanied by an able-bodied stranger. A few remarks passed between father and daughter, of which Dennistoun only caught these words, said by the sacristan, 'He was laughing in the church,' words which were answered only by a look of terror from the girl.

But in another minute they were in the sitting-room of the house, a small, high chamber with a stone floor, full of moving shadows cast by a wood-fire that flickered on a great hearth. Something of the character of an oratory was imparted to it by a tall crucifix, which reached almost to the ceiling on one side; the figure was painted of the natural colours, the cross was black. Under this stood a chest of some age and solidity, and when a lamp had been brought, and chairs set, the sacristan went to this chest, and produced therefrom, with growing excitement and nervousness, as Dennistoun thought, a large book, wrapped in a white cloth, on which cloth a cross was rudely embroidered in red thread. Even before the wrapping had been removed, Dennistoun began to be interested by the size and shape of the volume. 'Too large for a missal,' he thought, 'and not the shape of an antiphoner; perhaps it may be something good, after all.' The next moment the book was open, and Dennistoun felt that he had at last lit upon something better than good. Before him lay a large folio, bound, perhaps, late in the seventeenth century, with the arms of Canon Alberic de Mauléon stamped in gold on the sides. There may have been a hundred and fifty leaves of paper in the book, and on almost every one of them was fastened a leaf from an illuminated manuscript. Such a collection Dennistoun had hardly dreamed of in his wildest moments. Here were ten leaves from a copy of Genesis, illustrated with pictures, which could not be later than AD 700. Further on was a complete set of pictures from a Psalter, of English execution, of the very finest kind that the thirteenth century could produce; and, perhaps best of all, there were twenty leaves of uncial writing in Latin, which, as a few words seen here and there told him at once, must belong to some very early unknown patristic treatise. Could it possibly be a fragment of the copy of Papias 'On the Words of Our Lord', which was known to have existed as late as the twelfth century at Nîmes?* In any case, his mind was made up; that book must return to Cambridge with him, even if he had to draw the whole of his balance from the bank and stay at St Bertrand till the money came. He glanced up at the sacristan to see if his face yielded any hint that the book was for sale. The sacristan was pale, and his lips were working.

'If monsieur will turn on to the end,' he said.

So monsieur turned on, meeting new treasures at every rise of a leaf; and at the end of the book he came upon two sheets of paper, of much more recent date than anything he had yet seen, which puzzled him considerably. They must be contemporary, he decided, with the unprincipled Canon Alberic, who had doubtless plundered the Chapter library of St Bertrand to form this priceless scrap-book. On the first of the paper sheets was a plan, carefully drawn and instantly recognizable by a person who knew the ground, of the south

---

* We now know that these leaves did contain a considerable fragment of that work, if not of that actual copy of it.

aisle and cloisters of St Bertrand's. There were curious
signs looking like planetary symbols, and a few Hebrew words, in the corners; and in the north-west angle
of the cloister was a cross drawn in gold paint. Below
the plan were some lines of writing in Latin, which
ran thus:

Responsa 12^{mi} Dec. 1694. Interrogatum est: Inveniamne?
Responsum est: Invenies. Fiamne dives? Fies. Vivamne
invidendus? Vives. Moriarne in lecto meo? Ita. [Answers
of the 12th of December, 1694. It was asked: Shall I find
it? Answer: Thou shalt. Shall I become rich? Thou wilt.
Shall I live an object of envy? Thou wilt. Shall I die in
my bed? Thou wilt.]

'A good specimen of the treasure-hunter's record – quite
reminds one of Mr Minor-Canon Quatremain in *Old
St Paul's,*' was Dennistoun's comment, and he turned
the leaf.

What he then saw impressed him, as he has often
told me, more than he could have conceived any drawing
or picture capable of impressing him. And, though the
drawing he saw is no longer in existence, there is a photograph of it (which I possess) which fully bears out that
statement. The picture in question was a sepia drawing
at the end of the seventeenth century, representing, one

would say at first sight, a Biblical scene; for the architecture (the picture represented an interior) and the figures had that semi-classical flavour about them which the artists of two hundred years ago thought appropriate to illustrations of the Bible. On the right was a King on his throne, the throne elevated on twelve steps, a canopy overhead, lions on either side – evidently King Solomon. He was bending forward with outstretched sceptre, in attitude of command; his face expressed horror and disgust, yet there was in it also the mark of imperious will and confident power. The left half of the picture was the strangest, however. The interest plainly centred there. On the pavement before the throne were grouped four soldiers, surrounding a crouching figure which must be described in a moment. A fifth soldier lay dead on the pavement, his neck distorted, and his eyeballs starting from his head. The four surrounding guards were looking at the King. In their faces the sentiment of horror was intensified; they seemed, in fact, only restrained from flight by their implicit trust in their master. All this terror was plainly excited by the being that crouched in their midst. I entirely despair of conveying by any words the impression which this figure makes upon anyone who looks at it. I recollect once showing the photograph of the drawing to a lecturer on morphology – a person of, I was going to say, abnormally sane and unimaginative habits of mind. He absolutely refused to be alone for the rest of that evening, and he told me afterwards that for many nights he had not dared to put out his light before going to sleep. However, the main traits of the figure I can at least indicate. At first you saw only a mass of coarse, matted black hair; presently it was seen that this covered a body of fearful thinness, almost a skeleton, but with the muscles standing out like wires. The hands were of a dusky pallor, covered, like the body, with long, coarse hairs, and hideously taloned. The eyes, touched in with a burning yellow, had intensely black pupils, and were fixed upon the throned King with a look of beast-like hate. Imagine one of the awful bird-catching spiders of South America translated into human form, and endowed with intelligence just less than human, and you will have some faint conception of the terror inspired by this appalling effigy. One remark is universally made by those to whom I have shown the picture: 'It was drawn from the life.'

As soon as the first shock of his irresistible fright had subsided, Dennistoun stole a look at his hosts. The sacristan's hands were pressed upon his eyes; his daughter, looking up at the cross on the wall, was telling her beads feverishly.

At last the question was asked, 'Is this book for sale?'

There was the same hesitation, the same plunge of

determination that he had noticed before, and then came the welcome answer, 'If monsieur pleases.'

'How much do you ask for it?'

'I will take two hundred and fifty francs.'

This was confounding. Even a collector's conscience is sometimes stirred, and Dennistoun's conscience was tenderer than a collector's.

'My good man!' he said again and again, 'your book is worth far more than two hundred and fifty francs, I assure you – far more.'

But the answer did not vary: 'I will take two hundred and fifty francs, not more.'

There was really no possibility of refusing such a chance. The money was paid, the receipt signed, a glass of wine drunk over the transaction, and then the sacristan seemed to become a new man. He stood upright, he ceased to throw those suspicious glances behind him, he actually laughed or tried to laugh. Dennistoun rose to go.

'I shall have the honour of accompanying monsieur to his hotel?' said the sacristan.

'Oh no, thanks! it isn't a hundred yards. I know the way perfectly, and there is a moon.'

The offer was pressed three or four times, and refused as often.

'Then, monsieur will summon me if – if he finds

occasion; he will keep the middle of the road, the sides are so rough.'

'Certainly, certainly,' said Dennistoun, who was impatient to examine his prize by himself; and he stepped out into the passage with his book under his arm.

Here he was met by the daughter; she, it appeared, was anxious to do a little business on her own account; perhaps, like Gehazi, to 'take somewhat' from the foreigner whom her father had spared.

'A silver crucifix and chain for the neck; monsieur would perhaps be good enough to accept it?'

Well, really, Dennistoun hadn't much use for these things. What did mademoiselle want for it?

'Nothing – nothing in the world. Monsieur is more than welcome to it.'

The tone in which this and much more was said was unmistakably genuine, so that Dennistoun was reduced to profuse thanks, and submitted to have the chain put round his neck. It really seemed as if he had rendered the father and daughter some service which they hardly knew how to repay. As he set off with his book they stood at the door looking after him, and they were still looking when he waved them a last good night from the steps of the Chapeau Rouge.

Dinner was over, and Dennistoun was in his bedroom, shut up alone with his acquisition. The landlady had manifested a particular interest in him since he had told her that he had paid a visit to the sacristan and bought an old book from him. He thought, too, that he had heard a hurried dialogue between her and the said sacristan in the passage outside the *salle à manger*; some words to the effect that 'Pierre and Bertrand would be sleeping in the house' had closed the conversation.

All this time a growing feeling of discomfort had been creeping over him – nervous reaction, perhaps, after the delight of his discovery. Whatever it was, it resulted in a conviction that there was someone behind him, and that he was far more comfortable with his back to the wall. All this, of course, weighed light in the balance as against the obvious value of the collection he had acquired. And now, as I said, he was alone in his bedroom, taking stock of Canon Alberic's treasures, in which every moment revealed something more charming.

'Bless Canon Alberic!' said Dennistoun, who had an inveterate habit of talking to himself. 'I wonder where he is now? Dear me! I wish that landlady would learn to laugh in a more cheering manner; it makes one feel as if there was someone dead in the house. Half a pipe more, did you say? I think perhaps you are right. I wonder what that crucifix is that the young woman insisted on giving me? Last century, I suppose. Yes, probably. It is rather a nuisance of a thing to have round one's neck – just too heavy. Most likely her father has been wearing it for years. I think I might give it a clean up before I put it away.'

He had taken the crucifix off, and laid it on the table, when his attention was caught by an object lying on the red cloth just by his left elbow. Two or three ideas of what it might be flitted through his brain with their own incalculable quickness.

'A penwiper? No, no such thing in the house. A rat? No, too black. A large spider? I trust to goodness not – no. Good God! a hand like the hand in that picture!'

In another infinitesimal flash he had taken it in. Pale, dusky skin, covering nothing but bones and tendons of appalling strength; coarse black hairs, longer than ever grew on a human hand; nails rising from the ends of the fingers and curving sharply down and forward, grey, horny and wrinkled.

He flew out of his chair with deadly, inconceivable terror clutching at his heart. The shape, whose left hand rested on the table, was rising to a standing posture behind his seat, its right hand crooked above his scalp. There was black and tattered drapery about it; the coarse hair covered it as in the drawing. The lower jaw was thin – what can I call it? – shallow, like a beast's; teeth showed behind the black lips; there was no nose; the eyes, of a fiery yellow, against which the pupils showed black and intense, and the exulting hate and thirst to destroy life which shone there, were the most horrifying features in the whole vision. There was intelligence of a kind in them – intelligence beyond that of a beast, below that of a man.

The feelings which this horror stirred in Dennistoun were the intensest physical fear and the most profound mental loathing. What did he do? What could he do? He has never been quite certain what words he said, but he knows that he spoke, that he grasped blindly at the silver crucifix, that he was conscious of a movement towards him on the part of the demon, and that he screamed with the voice of an animal in hideous pain.

Pierre and Bertrand, the two sturdy little serving-men, who rushed in, saw nothing, but felt themselves thrust aside by something that passed out between them, and found Dennistoun in a swoon. They sat up with him that night, and his two friends were at St Bertrand by nine o'clock next morning. He himself, though still shaken and nervous, was almost himself by that time, and his story found credence with them, though not until they had seen the drawing and talked with the sacristan.

Almost at dawn the little man had come to the inn on some pretence, and had listened with the deepest interest to the story retailed by the landlady. He showed no surprise.

'It is he – it is he! I have seen him myself,' was his only comment; and to all questionings but one reply was vouchsafed: *'Deux fois je l'ai vu; mille fois j'ai senti.'* He would tell them nothing of the provenance of the book, nor any details of his experiences. 'I shall soon sleep, and my rest will be sweet. Why should you trouble me?' he said.*

We shall never know what he or Canon Alberic de Mauléon suffered. At the back of that fateful drawing were some lines of writing which may be supposed to throw light on the situation:

Contradictio Salomonis cum demonio nocturno.
Albericus de Mauleone delineavit.
V. Deus in adiutorium. Ps. Qui habitat.
Sancte Bertrande, demoniorium effugator, intercede
pro me miserrimo.
Primum uidi nocte 12^{mi} Dec. 1694: uidebo mox

---

* He died that summer; his daughter married, and settled at St Papoul. She never understood the circumstances of her father's 'obsession'.

ultimum. Peccaui et passus sum, plura adhuc
passurus. Dec. 29, 1701.*

I have never quite understood what was Dennistoun's
view of the events I have narrated. He quoted to me
once a text from Ecclesiasticus: 'Some spirits there be
that are created for vengeance, and in their fury lay on
sore strokes.' On another occasion he said: 'Isaiah was a
very sensible man; doesn't he say something about
night monsters living in the ruins of Babylon? These
things are rather beyond us at present.'

Another confidence of his impressed me rather, and
I sympathized with it. We had been, last year, to Comminges, to see Canon Alberic's tomb. It is a great marble
erection with an effigy of the Canon in a large wig and
soutane, and an elaborate eulogy of his learning below.
I saw Dennistoun talking for some time with the Vicar

* i.e., The Dispute of Solomon with a demon of the night. Drawn
by Alberic de Mauléon. *Versicle*. O Lord make haste to help me.
Psalm. Whoso dwelleth (xci).

Saint Bertrand, who puttest devils to flight, pray for me most
unhappy. I saw it first on the night of Dec. 12, 1694: soon I shall see
it for the last time. I have sinned and suffered, and have more to suf-
fer yet. Dec. 29, 1701

The 'Gallia Christiana' gives the date of the Canon's death as
December 31, 1701, 'in bed, of a sudden seizure'. Details of this
kind are not common in the great work of the Sammarthani.

of St Bertrand's, and as we drove away, he said to me: 'I hope it isn't wrong: you know I am a Presbyterian – but I – I believe there will be "saying of Mass and singing of dirges" for Alberic de Mauléon's rest.' Then he added, with a touch of the Northern British in his tone, 'I had no notion they came so dear.'

The book is in the Wentworth Collection at Cambridge. The drawing was photographed and then burnt by Dennistoun on the day when he left Comminges on the occasion of his first visit.

The Mezzotint

Some time ago I believe I had the pleasure of telling you the story of an adventure which happened to a friend of mine by the name of Dennistoun, during his pursuit of objects of art for the museum at Cambridge.

He did not publish his experiences very widely upon his return to England; but they could not fail to become known to a good many of his friends, and among others to the gentleman who at that time presided over an art museum at another University. It was to be expected that the story should make a considerable impression on the mind of a man whose vocation lay in lines similar to Dennistoun's, and that he should be eager to catch at any explanation of the matter which tended to make it seem improbable that he should ever be called upon to deal with so agitating an emergency. It was indeed, some-what consoling to him to reflect that he was not expected to acquire ancient MSS for his institution; that was the business of the Shelburnian Library. The authorities of that might, if they pleased, ransack obscure corners of the Continent for such matters. He was glad to be obliged at the moment to confine his attention to enlarging the already unsurpassed collection of English topographical drawings and engravings possessed by his museum. Yet, as it turned out, even a department so homely and familiar as this may have its dark corners, and to one of these Mr Williams was unexpectedly introduced.

Those who have taken even the most limited interest in the acquisition of topographical pictures are aware that there is one London dealer whose aid is indispensable to their researches. Mr J. W. Britnell publishes at short intervals very admirable catalogues of a large and constantly changing stock of engravings, plans, and old sketches of mansions, churches, and towns in England and Wales. These catalogues were, of course, the ABC of his subject to Mr Williams: but as his museum already contained an enormous accumulation of topographical pictures, he was a regular, rather than a copious, buyer; and he rather looked to Mr Britnell to fill up gaps in the rank and file of his collection than to supply him with rarities.

Now, in February of last year there appeared upon Mr Williams's desk at the museum a catalogue from Mr Britnell's emporium, and accompanying it was a typewritten communication from the dealer himself. This latter ran as follows:

Dear Sir, –

We beg to call your attention to No. 978 in our accompanying catalogue, which we shall be glad to send on approval.

Yours faithfully, J. W. Britnell

To turn to No. 978 in the accompanying catalogue was with Mr Williams (as he observed to himself) the work of a moment, and in the place indicated he found the following entry:

'978. – *Unknown*. Interesting mezzotint: View of a manor-house, early part of the century. 15 by 10 inches; black frame. £2 2s.'

It was not specially exciting, and the price seemed high. However, as Mr Britnell, who knew his business and his customer, seemed to set store by it, Mr Williams wrote a postcard asking for the article to be sent on approval, along with some other engravings and sketches which appeared in the same catalogue. And so he passed without much excitement of anticipation to the ordinary labours of the day.

A parcel of any kind always arrives a day later than you expect it, and that of Mr Britnell proved, as I believe the right phrase goes, no exception to the rule. It was delivered at the museum by the afternoon post of

Saturday, after Mr Williams had left his work, and it was accordingly brought round to his rooms in college by the attendant, in order that he might not have to wait over Sunday before looking through it and returning such of the contents as he did not propose to keep. And here he found it when he came in to tea, with a friend.

The only item with which I am concerned was the rather large, black-framed mezzotint of which I have already quoted the short description given in Mr Britnell's catalogue. Some more details of it will have to be given, though I cannot hope to put before you the look of the picture as clearly as it is present to my own eye. Very nearly the exact duplicate of it may be seen in a good many old inn parlours, or in the passages of undisturbed country mansions at the present moment. It was a rather indifferent mezzotint, and an indifferent mezzotint is, perhaps, the worst form of engraving known. It presented a full-face view of a not very large manor-house of the last century, with three rows of plain sashed windows with rusticated masonry about them, a parapet with balls or vases at the angles, and a small portico in the centre. On either side were trees, and in front a considerable expanse of lawn. The legend 'A. W. F. sculpsit' was engraved on the narrow margin; and there was no further inscription. The whole thing gave the impression that it was the work of an amateur. What in the world Mr Britnell could mean by affixing the price of £2 2s. to such an object was more than Mr Williams could imagine. He turned it over with a good deal of contempt; upon the back was a paper label, the left-hand half of which had been torn off. All that remained were the ends of two lines of writing: the first had the letters –*ngley Hall*; the second, –*ssex*.

It would, perhaps, be just worth while to identify the place represented, which he could easily do with the help of a gazetteer, and then he would send it back to Mr Britnell, with some remarks reflecting upon the judgement of that gentleman.

He lighted the candles, for it was now dark, made the tea, and supplied the friend with whom he had been play-ing golf (for I believe the authorities of the University I write of indulge in that pursuit by way of relaxation); and tea was taken to the accompaniment of a discussion which golfing persons can imagine for themselves, but which the conscientious writer has no right to inflict upon any non-golfing persons.

The conclusion arrived at was that certain strokes might have been better and that in certain emergencies neither player had experienced that amount of luck which a human being has a right to expect. It was now that the friend – let us call him Professor Binks – took up the framed engraving, and said:

'What's this place, Williams?'

'Just what I am going to try to find out,' said Williams, going to the shelf for a gazetteer. 'Look at the back. Somethingley Hall, either in Sussex or Essex. Half the name's gone, you see. You don't happen to know it, I suppose?'

'It's from that man Britnell, I suppose, isn't it?' said Binks. 'Is it for the museum?'

'Well, I think I should buy it if the price was five shillings,' said Williams, 'but for some unearthly reason he wants two guineas for it. I can't conceive why. It's a wretched engraving, and there aren't even any figures to give it life.'

'It's not worth two guineas, I should think,' said Binks; 'but I don't think it's so badly done. The moonlight seems rather good to me; and I should have thought there *were* figures, or at least a figure, just on the edge in front.'

'Let's look,' said Williams. 'Well, it's true the light is rather cleverly given. Where's your figure? Oh yes! Just the head, in the very front of the picture.'

And indeed there was – hardly more than a black blot on the extreme edge of the engraving – the head of a man or woman, a good deal muffled up, the back turned to the spectator, and looking towards the house.

Williams had not noticed it before.

'Still,' he said, 'though it's a cleverer thing than I thought, I can't spend two guineas of museum money on a picture of a place I don't know.'

Professor Binks had his work to do, and soon went; and very nearly up to Hall time Williams was engaged in a vain attempt to identify the subject of his picture. 'If the vowel before the *ng* had only been left, it would have been easy enough,' he thought; 'but as it is, the name may be anything from Guestingley to Langley, and there are many more names ending like this than I thought; and this rotten book has no index of terminations.'

Hall in Mr Williams's college was at seven. It need not be dwelt upon; the less so as he met there colleagues who had been playing golf during the afternoon, and words with which we have no concern were freely bandied across the table – merely golfing words, I would hasten to explain.

I suppose an hour or more to have been spent in what is called common-room after dinner. Later in the evening some few retired to Williams's rooms, and I have little doubt that whist was played and tobacco smoked. During a lull in these operations Williams

picked up the mezzotint from the table without looking at it, and handed it to a person mildly interested in
art, telling him where it had come from, and the other
particulars which we already know.

The gentleman took it carelessly, looked at it, then
said, in a tone of some interest:

'It's really a very good piece of work, Williams; it has
quite a feeling of the romantic period. The light is admi-
rably managed, it seems to me, and the figure, though
it's rather too grotesque, is somehow very impressive.'

'Yes, isn't it?' said Williams, who was just then busy
giving whisky-and-soda to others of the company, and
was unable to come across the room to look at the view
again.

It was by this time rather late in the evening, and the
visitors were on the move. After they went Williams
was obliged to write a letter or two and clear up some
odd bits of work. At last, some time past midnight, he
was disposed to turn in, and he put out his lamp after
lighting his bedroom candle. The picture lay face
upwards on the table where the last man who looked at
it had put it, and it caught his eye as he turned the lamp
down. What he saw made him very nearly drop the candle on the floor, and he declares now that if he had been
left in the dark at that moment he would have had a fit.
But, as that did not happen, he was able to put down the

light on the table and take a good look at the picture. It was indubitable – rankly impossible, no doubt, but absolutely certain. In the middle of the lawn in front of the unknown house there was a figure where no figure had been at five o'clock that afternoon. It was crawling on all-fours towards the house, and it was muffled in a strange black garment with a white cross on the back.

I do not know what is the ideal course to pursue in a situation of this kind. I can only tell you what Mr Williams did. He took the picture by one corner and carried it across the passage to a second set of rooms which he possessed. There he locked it up in a drawer, sported the doors of both sets of rooms, and retired to bed; but first he wrote out and signed an account of the extraordinary change which the picture had undergone since it had come into his possession.

Sleep visited him rather late; but it was consoling to reflect that the behaviour of the picture did not depend upon his own unsupported testimony. Evidently the man who had looked at it the night before had seen something of the same kind as he had, otherwise he might have been tempted to think that something gravely wrong was happening either to his eyes or his mind. This possibility being fortunately precluded, two matters awaited him on the morrow. He must take stock of the picture very carefully, and call in a witness for the purpose, and he must make a determined effort to ascertain what house it was that was represented. He would therefore ask his neighbour Nisbet to breakfast with him, and he would subsequently spend a morning over the gazetteer.

Nisbet was disengaged, and arrived about 9.30. His host was not quite dressed, I am sorry to say, even at this late hour. During breakfast nothing was said about the mezzotint by Williams, save that he had a picture on which he wished for Nisbet's opinion. But those who are familiar with University life can picture for themselves the wide and delightful range of subjects over which the conversation of two Fellows of Canterbury College is likely to extend during a Sunday morning breakfast. Hardly a topic was left unchallenged, from golf to lawn-tennis. Yet I am bound to say that Williams was rather distraught; for his interest naturally centred in that very strange picture which was now reposing, face downwards, in the drawer in the room opposite.

The morning pipe was at last lighted, and the moment had arrived for which he looked. With very considerable – almost tremulous – excitement he ran across, unlocked the drawer, and, extracting the picture – still face downwards – ran back, and put it into Nisbet's hands.

'Now,' he said, 'Nisbet, I want you to tell me exactly

what you see in that picture. Describe it, if you don't mind, rather minutely. I'll tell you why afterwards.'

'Well,' said Nisbet, 'I have here a view of a country-house – English, I presume – by moonlight.'

'Moonlight? You're sure of that?'

'Certainly. The moon appears to be on the wane, if you wish for details, and there are clouds in the sky.'

'All right. Go on. I'll swear,' added Williams in an aside, 'there was no moon when I saw it first.'

'Well, there's not much more to be said,' Nisbet continued. 'The house has one – two – three rows of windows, five in each row, except at the bottom, where there's a porch instead of the middle one, and –'

'But what about figures?' said Williams, with marked interest.

'There aren't any,' said Nisbet; 'but –'

'What! No figure on the grass in front?'

'Not a thing.'

'You'll swear to that?'

'Certainly I will. But there's just one other thing.'

'What?'

'Why, one of the windows on the ground floor – left of the door – is open.'

'Is it really? My goodness! he must have got in,' said Williams, with great excitement; and he hurried to the back of the sofa on which Nisbet was sitting, and catching the picture from him, verified the matter for himself.

It was quite true. There was no figure, and there was the open window. Williams, after a moment of speech-less surprise, went to the writing-table and scribbled for a short time. Then he brought two papers to Nisbet, and asked him first to sign one – it was his own descrip-tion of the picture, which you have just heard – and then to read the other which was Williams's statement written the night before.

'What can it all mean?' said Nisbet.

'Exactly,' said Williams. 'Well, one thing I must do – or three things, now I think of it. I must find out from Garwood' – this was his last night's visitor – 'what he saw, and then I must get the thing photographed before it goes further, and then I must find out what the place is.'

'I can do the photographing myself,' said Nisbet, 'and I will. But, you know, it looks very much as if we were assisting at the working out of a tragedy some-where. The question is, Has it happened already, or is it going to come off? You must find out what the place is. Yes,' he said, looking at the picture again, 'I expect you're right: he has got in. And if I don't mistake there'll be the devil to pay in one of the rooms upstairs.'

'I'll tell you what,' said Williams: 'I'll take the picture

across to old Green' (this was the senior Fellow of the College, who had been Bursar for many years). 'It's quite likely he'll know it. We have property in Essex and Sussex, and he must have been over the two counties a lot in his time.'

'Quite likely he will,' said Nisbet; 'but just let me take my photograph first. But look here, I rather think Green isn't up today. He wasn't in Hall last night, and I think I heard him say he was going down for the Sunday.'

'That's true, too,' said Williams; 'I know he's gone to Brighton. Well, if you'll photograph it now, I'll go across to Garwood and get his statement, and you keep an eye on it while I'm gone. I'm beginning to think two guineas is not a very exorbitant price for it now.'

In a short time he had returned, and brought Mr Garwood with him. Garwood's statement was to the effect that the figure, when he had seen it, was clear of the edge of the picture, but had not got far across the lawn. He remembered a white mark on the back of its drapery, but could not have been sure it was a cross. A document to this effect was then drawn up and signed, and Nisbet proceeded to photograph the picture.

'Now what do you mean to do?' he said. 'Are you going to sit and watch it all day?'

'Well, no, I think not,' said Williams. 'I rather imagine we're meant to see the whole thing. You see, between the time I saw it last night and this morning there was time for lots of things to happen, but the creature only got into the house. It could easily have got through its business in the time and gone to its own place again; but the fact of the window being open, I think, must mean that it's in there now. So I feel quite easy about leaving it. And, besides, I have a kind of idea that it wouldn't change much, if at all, in the daytime. We might go out for a walk this afternoon, and come in to tea, or whenever it gets dark. I shall leave it out on the table here, and sport the door. My skip can get in, but no one else.'

The three agreed that this would be a good plan; and, further, that if they spent the afternoon together they would be less likely to talk about the business to other people; for any rumour of such a transaction as was going on would bring the whole of the Phasmato-logical Society about their ears.

We may give them a respite until five o'clock.

At or near that hour the three were entering Williams's staircase. They were at first slightly annoyed to see that the door of his rooms was unsported; but in a moment it was remembered that on Sunday the skips came for orders an hour or so earlier than on week-days. However, a surprise was awaiting them. The first thing they saw was the picture leaning up against a pile of books on the table, as it had been left, and the next thing was Williams's skip, seated on a chair opposite, gazing at it with undisguised horror. How was this? Mr Filcher (the name is not my own invention) was a servant of considerable standing, and set the standard of etiquette to all his own college and to several neighbouring ones, and nothing could be more alien to his practice than to be found sitting on his master's chair, or appearing to take any particular notice of his master's furniture or pictures. Indeed, he seemed to feel this himself. He started violently when the three men came into the room, and got up with a marked effort. Then he said: 'I ask your pardon, sir, for taking such a freedom as to set down.'

'Not at all, Robert,' interposed Mr Williams. 'I was meaning to ask you some time what you thought of that picture.'

'Well, sir, of course I don't set up my opinion again yours, but it ain't the pictur I should 'ang where my little girl could see it, sir.'

'Wouldn't you, Robert? Why not?'

'No, sir. Why, the pore child, I recollect once she see a Door Bible, with pictures not 'alf what that is, and we'ad to set up with her three or four nights afterwards, if you'll believe me; and if she was to ketch a sight of this skelinton here, or whatever it is, carrying off the pore baby, she would be in a taking. You know 'ow it is with children; 'ow nervish they git with a little thing and all. But what I should say, it don't seem a right pictur to be laying about, sir, not where anyone that's liable to be startled could come on it. Should you be wanting anything this evening, sir? Thank you, sir.'

With these words the excellent man went to continue the round of his masters, and you may be sure the gentlemen whom he left lost no time in gathering round the engraving. There was the house, as before under the waning moon and the drifting clouds. The window that had been open was shut, and the figure was once more on the lawn: but not this time crawling cautiously on hands and knees. Now it was erect and stepping swiftly, with long strides, towards the front of the picture. The moon was behind it, and the black drapery hung down over its face so that only hints of that could be seen, and what was visible made the spectators profoundly thankful that they could see no more than a white dome-like forehead and a few straggling hairs. The head was bent down, and the arms were tightly clasped over an object which could be dimly seen and identified as a child, whether dead or living it was not possible to say. The legs of the appearance alone could be plainly discerned, and they were horribly thin.

From five to seven the three companions sat and

watched the picture by turns. But it never changed. They agreed at last that it would be safe to leave it, and that they would return after Hall and await further developments.

When they assembled again, at the earliest possible moment, the engraving was there, but the figure was gone, and the house was quiet under the moonbeams. There was nothing for it but to spend the evening over gazetteers and guide-books. Williams was the lucky one at last, and perhaps he deserved it. At 11.30 p.m. he read from Murray's *Guide to Essex* the following lines:

'16½ miles, *Anningley*. The church has been an interesting building of Norman date, but was extensively classicized in the last century. It contains the tombs of the family of Francis, whose mansion, Anningley Hall, a solid Queen Anne house, stands immediately beyond the churchyard in a park of about 80 acres. The family is now extinct, the last heir having disappeared mysteriously in infancy in the year 1802. The father, Mr Arthur Francis, was locally known as a talented amateur engraver in mezzotint. After his son's disappearance he lived in complete retirement at the Hall, and was found dead in his studio on the third anniversary of the disaster, having just completed an engraving of the house, impressions of which are of considerable rarity.'

This looked like business, and, indeed, Mr Green on his return at once identified the house as Anningley Hall.

'Is there any kind of explanation of the figure, Green?' was the question which Williams naturally asked.

'I don't know, I'm sure, Williams. What used to be said in the place when I first knew it, which was before I came up here, was just this: old Francis was always very much down on these poaching fellows, and whenever he got a chance he used to get a man whom he suspected of it turned off the estate, and by degrees he got rid of them all but one. Squires could do a lot of things then that they daren't think of now. Well, this man that was left was what you find pretty often in that country – the last remains of a very old family. I believe they were Lords of the Manor at one time. I recollect just the same thing in my own parish.'

'What, like the man in *Tess of the D'Urbervilles?*' Williams put in.

'Yes, I dare say; it's not a book I could ever read myself. But this fellow could show a row of tombs in the church there that belonged to his ancestors, and all that went to sour him a bit; but Francis, they said, could never get at him – he always kept just on the right side of the law – until one night the keepers found him at it in a wood right at the end of the estate. I could show you the place now; it marches with some land that used to belong to an uncle of mine. And you can imagine there was a row; and this man Gawdy (that was the name, to be sure – Gawdy; I thought I should get it – Gawdy), he was unlucky enough, poor chap! to shoot a keeper. Well, that was what Francis wanted, and grand juries – you know what they would have been then – and poor Gawdy was strung up in double-quick time; and I've been shown the place he was buried in, on the north side of the church – you know the way in that part of the world: anyone that's been hanged or made away with themselves, they bury them that side. And the idea was that some friend of Gawdy's – not a relation, because he had none, poor devil! he was the last of his line: kind of *spes ultima gentis* – must have planned to get hold of Francis's boy and put an end to *his* line, too. I don't know – it's rather an out-of-the-way thing for an Essex poacher to think of – but, you know, I should say now it looks more as if old Gawdy had managed the job himself. Booh! I hate to think of it! Have some whisky, Williams!'

The facts were communicated by Williams to Dennistoun, and by him to a mixed company, of which I was one, and the Sadducean Professor of Ophiology another. I am sorry to say that the latter, when asked what he thought of it, only remarked: 'Oh, those Bridgeford people will say anything' – a sentiment which met with the reception it deserved.

I have only to add that the picture is now in the Ashleian Museum; that it has been treated with a view to discovering whether sympathetic ink has been used in it, but without effect; that Mr Britnell knew nothing of it save that he was sure it was uncommon; and that, though carefully watched, it has never been known to change again.

The Rose Garden

Mr and Mrs Anstruther were at breakfast in the parlour of Westfield Hall, in the county of Essex. They were arranging plans for the day.

'George,' said Mrs Anstruther, 'I think you had better take the car to Maldon and see if you can get any of those knitted things I was speaking about which would do for my stall at the bazaar.'

'Oh well, if you wish it, Mary, of course I can do that, but I had half arranged to play a round with Geoffrey Williamson this morning. The bazaar isn't till Thursday of next week, is it?'

'What has that to do with it, George? I should have thought you would have guessed that if I can't get the things I want in Maldon I shall have to write to all manner of shops in town: and they are certain to send something quite unsuitable in price or quality the first time. If you have actually made an appointment with

Mr Williamson, you had better keep it, but I must say I think you might have let me know.'

'Oh no, no, it wasn't really an appointment. I quite see what you mean. I'll go. And what shall you do yourself?'

'Why, when the work of the house is arranged for, I must see about laying out my new rose garden. By the way, before you start for Maldon I wish you would just take Collins to look at the place I fixed upon. You know it, of course.'

'Well, I'm not quite sure that I do, Mary. Is it at the upper end, towards the village?'

'Good gracious no, my dear George; I thought I had made that quite clear. No, it's that small clearing just off the shrubbery path that goes towards the church.'

'Oh yes, where we were saying there must have been a summer-house once: the place with the old seat and the posts. But do you think there's enough sun there?'

'My dear George, do allow me *some* common sense, and don't credit me with all your ideas about summer-houses. Yes, there will be plenty of sun when we have got rid of some of those box-bushes. I know what you are going to say, and I have as little wish as you to strip the place bare. All I want Collins to do is to clear away the old seats and the posts and things before I come out in an hour's time. And I hope you will manage to get off fairly soon. After luncheon I think I shall go on with my sketch of the church; and if you please you can go over to the links, or –'

'Ah, a good idea – very good! Yes, you finish that sketch, Mary, and I should be glad of a round.'

'I was going to say, you might call on the Bishop; but I suppose it is no use my making *any* suggestion. And now do be getting ready, or half the morning will be gone.'

Mr Anstruther's face, which had shown symptoms of lengthening, shortened itself again, and he hurried from the room, and was soon heard giving orders in the passage. Mrs Anstruther, a stately dame of some fifty summers, proceeded, after a second consideration of the morning's letters, to her housekeeping.

Within a few minutes Mr Anstruther had discovered Collins in the greenhouse, and they were on their way to the site of the projected rose garden. I do not know much about the conditions most suitable to these nurseries, but I am inclined to believe that Mrs Anstruther, though in the habit of describing herself as 'a great gardener', had not been well advised in the selection of a spot for the purpose. It was a small, dank clearing, bounded on one side by a path, and on the other by thick box-bushes, laurels, and other evergreens. The ground was almost bare of grass and dark of aspect. Remains of rustic seats and an old and corrugated oak post somewhere near the middle of the clearing had given rise to Mr Anstruther's conjecture that a summer-house had once stood there.

Clearly Collins had not been put in possession of his mistress's intentions with regard to this plot of ground: and when he learnt them from Mr Anstruther he displayed no enthusiasm.

'Of course I could clear them seats away soon enough,' he said. 'They aren't no ornament to the place, Mr Anstruther, and rotten too. Look 'ere, sir' – and he broke off a large piece – 'rotten right through. Yes, clear them away, to be sure we can do that.'

'And the post,' said Mr Anstruther, 'that's got to go too.'

Collins advanced, and shook the post with both hands: then he rubbed his chin.

'That's firm in the ground, that post is,' he said. 'That's been there a number of years, Mr Anstruther. I doubt I shan't get that up not quite so soon as what I can do with them seats.'

'But your mistress specially wishes it to be got out of the way in an hour's time,' said Mr Anstruther.

Collins smiled and shook his head slowly. 'You'll excuse me, sir, but you feel of it for yourself. No, sir, no one can't do what's impossible to 'em, can they, sir? I could git that post up by after tea-time, sir, but that'll want a lot of digging. What you require, you see, sir, if you'll excuse me naming of it, you want the soil loosening round this post 'ere, and me and the boy we shall take a little time doing of that. But now, these 'ere seats,' said Collins, appearing to appropriate this portion of the scheme as due to his own resourcefulness, 'why, I can get the barrer round and 'ave them cleared away in, why less than an hour's time from now, if you'll permit of it. Only –'

'Only what, Collins?'

'Well now, it ain't for me to go against orders no more than what it is for you yourself – or anyone else' (this was added somewhat hurriedly), 'but if you'll pardon me, sir, this ain't the place I should have picked out for no rose garden myself. Why look at them box and laurestinus, 'ow they reg'lar preclude the light from –'

'Ah yes, but we've got to get rid of some of them, of course.'

'Oh, indeed, get rid of them! Yes, to be sure, but – I beg your pardon, Mr Anstruther –'

'I'm sorry, Collins, but I must be getting on now. I hear the car at the door. Your mistress will explain exactly what she wishes. I'll tell her, then, that you can see your way to clearing away the seats at once, and the post this afternoon. Good morning.'

Collins was left rubbing his chin. Mrs Anstruther

received the report with some discontent, but did not insist upon any change of plan.

By four o'clock that afternoon she had dismissed her husband to his golf, had dealt faithfully with Collins and with the other duties of the day, and, having sent a campstool and umbrella to the proper spot, had just settled down to her sketch of the church as seen from the shrubbery, when a maid came hurrying down the path to report that Miss Wilkins had called.

Miss Wilkins was one of the few remaining members of the family from whom the Anstruthers had bought the Westfield estate some few years back. She had been staying in the neighbourhood, and this was probably a farewell visit. 'Perhaps you could ask Miss Wilkins to join me here,' said Mrs Anstruther, and soon Miss Wilkins, a person of mature years, approached.

'Yes, I'm leaving the Ashes tomorrow, and I shall be able to tell my brother how tremendously you have improved the place. Of course he can't help regretting the old house just a little – as I do myself – but the garden is really delightful now.'

'I am so glad you can say so. But you mustn't think we've finished our improvements. Let me show you where I mean to put a rose garden. It's close by here.'

The details of the project were laid before Miss Wilkins

at some length; but her thoughts were evidently else-where.

'Yes, delightful,' she said at last rather absently. 'But do you know, Mrs Anstruther, I'm afraid I was thinking of old times. I'm *very* glad to have seen just this spot again before you altered it. Frank and I had quite a romance about this place.'

'Yes?' said Mrs Anstruther smilingly; 'do tell me what it was. Something quaint and charming, I'm sure.'

'Not so very charming, but it has always seemed to me curious. Neither of us would ever be here alone when we were children, and I'm not sure that I should care about it now in certain moods. It is one of those things that can hardly be put into words – by me at least – and that sound rather foolish if they are not prop-erly expressed. I can tell you after a fashion what it was that gave us – well, almost a horror of the place when we were alone. It was towards the evening of one very hot autumn day, when Frank had disappeared mysteri-ously about the grounds, and I was looking for him to fetch him to tea, and going down this path I suddenly saw him, not hiding in the bushes, as I rather expected, but sitting on the bench in the old summer-house – there was a wooden summer-house here, you know – up in the corner, asleep, but with such a dreadful look on his

49

face that I really thought he must be ill or even dead. I rushed at him and shook him, and told him to wake up; and wake up he did, with a scream. I assure you the poor boy seemed almost beside himself with fright. He hurried me away to the house, and was in a terrible state all that night, hardly sleeping. Someone had to sit up with him, as far as I remember. He was better very soon, but for days I couldn't get him to say why he had been in such a condition. It came out at last that he had really been asleep and had had a very odd disjointed sort of dream. He never *saw* much of what was around him, but he *felt* the scenes most vividly. First he made out that he was standing in a large room with a number of people in it, and that someone was opposite to him who was "very powerful", and he was being asked questions which he felt to be very important, and, whenever he answered them, someone – either the person opposite to him, or someone else in the room – seemed to be, as he said, making something up against him. All the voices sounded to him very distant, but he remembered bits of the things that were said: "Where were you on the 19th of October?" and "Is this your handwriting?" and so on. I can see now, of course, that he was dreaming of some trial: but we were never allowed to see the papers, and it was odd that a boy of eight should have such a vivid idea of what went on in a court. All the time he felt, he said,

the most intense anxiety and oppression and hopeless-
ness (though I don't suppose he used such words as that
to me). Then, after that, there was an interval in which
he remembered being dreadfully restless and miserable,
and then there came another sort of picture, when he
was aware that he had come out of doors on a dark raw
morning with a little snow about. It was in a street, or at
any rate among houses, and he felt that there were numbers and numbers of people there too, and that he was
taken up some creaking wooden steps and stood on a
sort of platform, but the only thing he could actually see
was a small fire burning somewhere near him. Someone
who had been holding his arm left hold of it and went
towards this fire, and then he said the fright he was in
was worse than at any other part of his dream, and if I
had not wakened him up he didn't know what would
have become of him. A curious dream for a child to
have, wasn't it? Well, so much for that. It must have been
later in the year that Frank and I were here, and I was
sitting in the arbour just about sunset. I noticed the sun
was going down, and told Frank to run in and see if tea
was ready while I finished a chapter in the book I was
reading. Frank was away longer than I expected, and the
light was going so fast that I had to bend over my book
to make it out. All at once I became conscious that someone was whispering to me inside the arbour. The only

words I could distinguish, or thought I could, were something like "Pull, pull. I'll push, you pull."

'I started up in something of a fright. The voice – it was little more than a whisper – sounded so hoarse and angry, and yet as if it came from a long, long way off – just as it had done in Frank's dream. But, though I was startled, I had enough courage to look round and try to make out where the sound came from. And – this sounds very foolish, I know, but still it is the fact – I made sure that it was strongest when I put my ear to an old post which was part of the end of the seat. I was so certain of this that I remember making some marks on the post – as deep as I could with the scissors out of my work-basket. I don't know why. I wonder, by the way, whether that isn't the very post itself . . . Well, yes, it might be: there *are* marks and scratches on it – but one can't be sure. Anyhow, it was just like that post you have there. My father got to know that both of us had had a fright in the arbour, and he went down there himself one evening after dinner, and the arbour was pulled down at very short notice. I recollect hearing my father talking about it to an old man who used to do odd jobs in the place, and the old man saying, "Don't you fear for that, sir: he's fast enough in there without no one don't take and let him out." But when I asked who it was, I could get no satisfactory answer. Possibly my father or mother might have told me more about it when I grew up, but, as you know, they both died when we were still quite children. I must say it has always seemed very odd to me, and I've often asked the older people in the village whether they knew of anything strange: but either they knew nothing or they wouldn't tell me. Dear, dear, how I have been boring you with my childish remembrances! but indeed that arbour did absorb our thoughts quite remarkably for a time. You can fancy, can't you, the kind of stories that we made up for ourselves. Well, dear Mrs Anstruther, I must be leaving you now. We shall meet in town this winter, I hope, shan't we?' etc., etc.

The seats and the post were cleared away and uprooted respectively by that evening. Late summer weather is proverbially treacherous, and during dinner-time Mrs Collins sent up to ask for a little brandy, because her husband had took a nasty chill and she was afraid he would not be able to do much next day.

Mrs Anstruther's morning reflections were not wholly placid. She was sure some roughs had got into the plantation during the night. 'And another thing, George: the moment that Collins is about again, you must tell him to do something about the owls. I never heard anything like them, and I'm positive one came and perched somewhere just outside our window. If it had come in I should have been out of my wits: it must have been a very large bird, from its voice. Didn't you hear it? No, of course not, you were sound asleep as usual. Still, I must say, George, you don't look as if your night had done you much good.'

'My dear, I feel as if another of the same would turn me silly. You have no idea of the dreams I had. I couldn't speak of them when I woke up, and if this room wasn't so bright and sunny I shouldn't care to think of them even now.'

'Well, really, George, that isn't very common with you, I must say. You must have – no, you only had what I had yesterday – unless you had tea at that wretched club house: did you?'

'No, no; nothing but a cup of tea and some bread and butter. I should really like to know how I came to put my dream together – as I suppose one does put one's dreams together from a lot of little things one has been seeing or reading. Look here, Mary, it was like this – if I shan't be boring you –'

'I *wish* to hear what it was, George. I will tell you when I have had enough.'

'All right. I must tell you that it wasn't like other nightmares in one way, because I didn't really *see* anyone who spoke to me or touched me, and yet I was most fearfully impressed with the reality of it all. First I was sitting, no, moving about, in an old-fashioned sort

of panelled room. I remember there was a fireplace and
a lot of burnt papers in it, and I was in a great state of
anxiety about something. There was someone else – a
servant, I suppose, because I remember saying to him,
"Horses, as quick as you can," and then waiting a bit: and
next I heard several people coming upstairs and a noise
like spurs on a boarded floor, and then the door opened
and whatever it was that I was expecting happened.'

'Yes, but what was that?'

'You see, I couldn't tell: it was the sort of shock that
upsets you in a dream. You either wake up or else everything goes black. That was what happened to me. Then I
was in a big dark-walled room, panelled, I think, like the
other, and a number of people, and I was evidently –'

'Standing your trial, I suppose, George.'

'Goodness! yes, Mary, I was; but did you dream that
too? How very odd!'

'No, no; I didn't get enough sleep for that. Go on,
George, and I will tell you afterwards.'

'Yes; well, I *was* being tried, for my life, I've no doubt,
from the state I was in. I had no one speaking for me,
and somewhere there was a most fearful fellow – on the
bench, I should have said, only that he seemed to be
pitching into me most unfairly, and twisting everything
I said, and asking most abominable questions.'

'What about?'

'Why, dates when I was at particular places, and letters I was supposed to have written, and why I had destroyed some papers; and I recollect his laughing at answers I made in a way that quite daunted me. It doesn't sound much, but I can tell you, Mary, it was really appalling at the time. I am quite certain there was such a man once, and a most horrible villain he must have been. The things he said –'

'Thank you, I have no wish to hear them. I can go to the links any day myself. How did it end?'

'Oh, against me; *he* saw to that. I do wish, Mary, I could give you a notion of the strain that came after that, and seemed to me to last for days: waiting and waiting, and sometimes writing things I knew to be enormously important to me, and waiting for answers and none coming, and after that I came out –'

'Ah!'

'What makes you say that? Do you know what sort of thing I saw?'

'Was it a dark cold day, and snow in the streets, and a fire burning somewhere near you?'

'By George, it was! You *have* had the same nightmare! Really not? Well, it is the oddest thing! Yes; I've no doubt it was an execution for high treason. I know I was laid on straw and jolted along most wretchedly, and then had to go up some steps, and someone was holding my arm, and I remember seeing a bit of a ladder and hearing a sound of a lot of people. I really don't think I could bear now to go into a crowd of people and hear the noise they make talking. However, mercifully, I didn't get to the real business. The dream passed off with a sort of thunder inside my head. But, Mary –'

'I know what you are going to ask. I suppose this is an instance of a kind of thought-reading. Miss Wilkins called yesterday and told me of a dream her brother had as a child when they lived here, and something did no doubt make me think of that when I was awake last night listening to those horrible owls and those men talking and laughing in the shrubbery (by the way, I wish you would see if they have done any damage, and speak to the police about it); and so, I suppose, from my brain it must have got into yours while you were asleep. Curious, no doubt, and I am sorry it gave you such a bad night. You had better be as much in the fresh air as you can today.'

'Oh, it's all right now; but I think I *will* go over to the Lodge and see if I can get a game with any of them. And you?'

'I have enough to do for this morning; and this afternoon, if I am not interrupted, there is my drawing.'

'To be sure – I want to see that finished very much.'

No damage was discoverable in the shrubbery.

Mr Anstruther surveyed with faint interest the site of the rose garden, where the uprooted post still lay, and the hole it had occupied remained unfilled. Collins, upon inquiry made, proved to be better, but quite unable to come to his work. He expressed, by the mouth of his wife, a hope that he hadn't done nothing wrong clearing away them things. Mrs Collins added that there was a lot of talking people in Westfield, and the hold ones was the worst: seemed to think everything of them having been in the parish longer than what other people had. But as to what they said no more could then be ascertained than that it had quite upset Collins, and was a lot of nonsense.

Recruited by lunch and a brief period of slumber, Mrs Anstruther settled herself comfortably upon her sketching chair in the path leading through the shrubbery to the side-gate of the churchyard. Trees and buildings were among her favourite subjects, and here she had good studies of both. She worked hard, and the drawing was becoming a really pleasant thing to look upon by the time that the wooded hills to the west had shut off the sun. Still she would have persevered, but the light changed rapidly, and it became obvious that the last touches must be added on the morrow. She rose and turned towards the house, pausing for a time to take delight in the limpid green western sky. Then she passed on between the dark box-bushes, and, at a point just before the path debouched on the lawn, she stopped once again and considered the quiet evening landscape, and made a mental note that that must be the tower of one of the Roothing churches that one caught on the sky-line. Then a bird (perhaps) rustled in the box-bush on her left, and she turned and started at seeing what at first she took to be a Fifth of November mask peeping out among the branches. She looked closer.

It was not a mask. It was a face – large, smooth, and pink. She remembers the minute drops of perspiration which were starting from its forehead: she remembers how the jaws were clean-shaven and the eyes shut. She remembers also, and with an accuracy which makes the thought intolerable to her, how the mouth was open and a single tooth appeared below the upper lip. As she looked the face receded into the darkness of the bush. The shelter of the house was gained and the door shut before she collapsed.

Mr and Mrs Anstruther had been for a week or more recruiting at Brighton before they received a circular from the Essex Archaeological Society, and a query as to whether they possessed certain historical portraits which it was desired to include in the forthcoming work on Essex Portraits, to be published under the Society's auspices. There was an accompanying letter from the Secretary which contained the following passage: 'We are specially anxious to know whether you possess the original of the engraving of which I enclose a photograph. It represents Sir —, Lord Chief Justice under Charles II, who, as you doubtless know, retired after his disgrace to Westfield, and is supposed to have died there of remorse. It may interest you to hear that a curious entry has recently been found in the registers, not of Westfield but of Priors Roothing, to the effect that the parish was so much troubled after his death that the rector of Westfield summoned the parsons of all the Roothings to come and lay him; which they did. The entry ends by saying: "The stake is in a field adjoining to the churchyard of Westfield, on the west side." Perhaps you can let us know if any tradition to this effect is current in your parish.'

The incidents which the 'enclosed photograph' recalled were productive of a severe shock to Mrs Anstruther. It was decided that she must spend the winter abroad.

Mr Anstruther, when he went down to Westfield to make the necessary arrangements, not unnaturally told his story to the rector (an old gentleman), who showed little surprise.

'Really I had managed to piece out for myself very

much what must have happened, partly from old people's talk and partly from what I saw in your grounds. Of course we have suffered to some extent also. Yes, it was bad at first: like owls, as you say, and men talking sometimes. One night it was in this garden, and at other times about several of the cottages. But lately there has been very little: I think it will die out. There is nothing in our registers except the entry of the burial, and what I for a long time took to be the family motto; but last time I looked at it I noticed that it was added in a later hand and had the initials of one of our rectors quite late in the seventeenth century, A. C. – Augustine Crompton. Here it is, you see – *quieta non movere*. I suppose – Well, it is rather hard to say exactly what I do suppose.'

The Stalls of Barchester Cathedral

This matter began, as far as I am concerned, with the reading of a notice in the obituary section of the *Gentleman's Magazine* for an early year in the nineteenth century:

'On February 26th, at his residence in the Cathedral Close of Barchester, the Venerable John Benwell Haynes, D. D., aged 57, Archdeacon of Sowerbridge and Rector of Pickhill and Candley. He was of — College, Cambridge, and where, by talent and assiduity, he commanded the esteem of his seniors; when, at the usual time, he took his first degree, his name stood high in the list of *wranglers*. These academical honours procured for him within a short time a Fellowship of his College. In the year 1783 he received Holy Orders, and was shortly afterwards presented to the perpetual Curacy of Ranxton-sub-Ashe by his friend and patron the late truly venerable Bishop of Lichfield . . . His speedy preferments, first to a Prebend, and subsequently to the dignity of Precentor in the Cathedral of Barchester, form an eloquent testimony to the respect in which he was held and to his eminent qualifications. He succeeded to the Archdeaconry upon the sudden decease of Archdeacon Pulteney in 1810. His sermons, ever conformable to the principles of the religion and Church which he adorned, displayed in no ordinary degree, without the least trace of enthusiasm, the refinement of the scholar united with the graces of the Christian. Free from sectarian violence, and informed by the spirit of the truest charity, they will long dwell in the memories of his hearers. (Here a further omission.) The productions of his pen include an able defence of Episcopacy, which, though often perused by the author of this tribute to his memory, afford but one additional instance of the want of liberality and enterprise which is a too common characteristic of the publishers of our generation. His published works are, indeed, confined to a spirited and elegant version of the *Argonautica* of Valerius Flaccus, a volume of *Discourses upon the Several Events in the Life of Joshua*, delivered in his Cathedral, and a number of the charges which he pronounced at various visitations to the clergy of his Archdeaconry. These are distinguished by etc., etc. The urbanity and hospitality of the subject of these lines will not readily be forgotten by those who enjoyed his acquaintance. His interest in the venerable and awful pile under whose hoary vault he was so punctual an attendant, and particularly in the musical portion of its rites, might be termed filial, and formed a strong and delightful contrast to the polite indifference displayed by too many of our Cathedral dignitaries at the present time.'

The final paragraph, after informing us that Dr Haynes died a bachelor, says:

'It might have been augured that an existence so placid and benevolent would have been terminated in a ripe old age by a dissolution equally gradual and calm. But how unsearchable are the workings of Providence! The peaceful and retired seclusion amid which the honoured evening of Dr Haynes's life was mellowing to its close was destined to be disturbed, nay, shattered, by a tragedy as appalling as it was unexpected. The morning of the 26th of February –'

But perhaps I shall do better to keep back the remainder of the narrative until I have told the circumstances which led up to it. These, as far as they are now accessible, I have derived from another source.

I had read the obituary notice which I have been quoting, quite by chance, along with a great many others of the same period. It had excited some little speculation in my mind, but, beyond thinking that, if I ever had an opportunity of examining the local records of the period indicated, I would try to remember Dr Haynes, I made no effort to pursue his case.

Quite lately I was cataloguing the manuscripts in the library of the college to which he belonged. I had reached the end of the numbered volumes on the shelves, and I proceeded to ask the librarian whether there were any more books which he thought I ought to include in my description. 'I don't think there are,' he said, 'but we had better come and look at the manuscript class and make sure. Have you time to do that now?' I had time. We went to the library, checked off the manuscripts, and, at the end of our survey, arrived at a shelf of which I had seen nothing. Its contents consisted for the most part of sermons, bundles of fragmentary papers, college exercises, *Cyrus*, an epic poem in several cantos, the product of a country clergyman's leisure, mathematical tracts by a deceased professor, and other similar material of a kind with which I am only too familiar. I took brief notes of these. Lastly, there was a tin box, which was pulled out and dusted. Its label, much faded, was thus inscribed: 'Papers of the Ven. Archdeacon Haynes. Bequeathed in 1834 by his sister, Miss Letitia Haynes.'

I knew at once that the name was one which I had somewhere encountered, and could very soon locate it. 'That must be the Archdeacon Haynes who came to a very odd end at Barchester. I've read his obituary in the *Gentleman's Magazine*. May I take the box home? Do you know if there is anything interesting in it?'

The librarian was very willing that I should take the box and examine it at leisure. 'I never looked inside it myself,' he said, 'but I've always been meaning to. I am pretty sure that is the box which our old Master once said ought never to have been accepted by the college. He said that to Martin years ago; and he said also that as long as he had control over the library it should never be opened. Martin told me about it, and said that he wanted terribly to know what was in it; but the Master was librarian, and always kept the box in the lodge, so there was no getting at it in his time; and when he died it was taken away by mistake by his heirs, and only returned a few years ago. I can't think why I haven't opened it; but, as I have to go away from Cambridge this afternoon, you had better have first go at it. I think I can trust you not to publish anything undesirable in our catalogue.'

I took the box home and examined its contents, and thereafter consulted the librarian as to what should be done about publication, and, since I have his leave to make a story out of it, provided I disguise the identity of the people concerned, I will try what can be done.

The materials are, of course, mainly journals and letters. How much I shall quote and how much epitomize must be determined by considerations of space. The proper understanding of the situation has necessitated a little – not very arduous – research, which has been greatly facilitated by the excellent illustrations and text of the Barchester volume in Bell's *Cathedral Series*.

When you enter the choir of Barchester Cathedral now, you pass through a screen of metal and coloured marbles, designed by Sir Gilbert Scott, and find yourself in what I must call a very bare and odiously furnished place. The stalls are modern, without canopies. The places of the dignitaries and the names of the prebends have fortunately been allowed to survive, and are inscribed on small brass plates affixed to the stalls. The organ is in the triforium, and what is seen of the case is Gothic. The reredos and its surroundings are like every other.

Careful engravings of a hundred years ago show a very different state of things. The organ is on a massive classical screen. The stalls are also classical and very massive. There is a baldacchino of wood over the altar, with urns upon its corners. Farther east is a solid altar screen, classical in design, of wood, with a pediment, in which is a triangle surrounded by rays, enclosing certain Hebrew letters in gold. Cherubs contemplate these. There is a pulpit with a great sounding-board at the eastern end of the stalls on the north side, and there is a black and white marble pavement. Two ladies and a gentleman are admiring the general effect. From other sources I gather that the archdeacon's stall then, as now, was next to the bishop's throne at the south-eastern end of the stalls. His house almost faces the west front of the church, and is a fine red-brick building of William the Third's time.

Here Dr Haynes, already a mature man, took up his abode with his sister in the year 1810. The dignity had long been the object of his wishes, but his predecessor refused to depart until he had attained the age of ninety-two. About a week after he had held a modest festival in celebration of that ninety-second birthday, there came a morning, late in the year, when Dr Haynes, hurrying cheerfully into his breakfast-room, rubbing his hands and humming a tune, was greeted, and checked in his genial flow of spirits, by the sight of his sister, seated, indeed, in her usual place behind the tea-urn, but bowed forward and sobbing unrestrainedly into her handkerchief. 'What – what is the matter? What bad news?' he began. 'Oh, Johnny, you've not heard? The poor dear archdeacon!' 'The archdeacon, yes? What is it – ill, is he?' 'No, no; they found him on the staircase this morning; it is so shocking.' 'Is it possible! Dear, dear, poor Pulteney! Had there been any seizure?' 'They don't think so, and that is almost the worst thing about it. It seems to have been all the fault of that stupid maid of theirs, Jane.' Dr Haynes paused. 'I don't quite understand, Letitia. How was the maid at fault?' 'Why, as far as I can make out, there was a stair-rod missing, and she never mentioned it, and the poor archdeacon set his foot quite on the edge of the step – you know how slippery that oak is – and it seems he must have fallen almost the whole flight and broken his neck. It *is* so sad for poor Miss Pulteney. Of course, they will get rid of the girl at once. I never liked her.' Miss Haynes's grief resumed its sway, but eventually relaxed so far as to permit of her taking some breakfast. Not so her brother, who, after standing in silence before the window for some minutes, left the room, and did not appear again that morning. I need only add that the careless maid-servant was dismissed forthwith, but that the missing stair-rod was very shortly afterwards found *under* the stair-carpet – an additional proof, if any were needed, of extreme stupidity and carelessness on her part.

For a good many years Dr Haynes had been marked out by his ability, which seems to have been really considerable, as the likely successor of Archdeacon Pulteney, and no disappointment was in store for him. He was duly installed, and entered with zeal upon the discharge of those functions which are appropriate to one in his position. A considerable space in his journals is occupied with exclamations upon the confusion in which Archdeacon Pulteney had left the business of his office and the documents appertaining to it. Dues upon Wringham and Barnswood have been uncollected for something like twelve years, and are largely irrecoverable; no visitation has been held for seven years; four chancels are almost past mending. The persons deputized by the archdeacon have been nearly as incapable as himself. It was almost a matter for thankfulness that this state of things had not been permitted to continue, and a letter from a friend confirms this view. ' "ὁ κατέχων,", ' it says (in rather cruel allusion to the Second Epistle to the Thessalonians), 'is removed at last. My poor friend! Upon what a scene of confusion will you be entering! I give you my word that, on the last occasion of my crossing his threshold, there was no single paper that he could lay hands upon, no syllable of mine that he could hear, and no fact in connection with my business that he could remember. But now, thanks to a negligent maid and a loose stair-carpet, there is some prospect that necessary business will be transacted without a complete loss alike of voice and temper.' This letter was tucked into a pocket in the cover of one of the diaries.

There can be no doubt of the new archdeacon's zeal and enthusiasm. 'Give me but time to reduce to some semblance of order the innumerable errors and complications with which I am confronted, and I shall gladly and sincerely join with the aged Israelite in the canticle which too many, I fear, pronounce but with their lips.' This reflection I find, not in a diary, but a letter; the doctor's friends seem to have returned his correspondence to his surviving sister. He does not confine himself, however, to reflections. His investigations of the rights and duties of his office are very searching and business-like, and there is a calculation in one place that a period of three years will just suffice to set the business of the Archdeaconry upon a proper footing. The estimate appears to have been an exact one. For just three years he is occupied in reforms; but I look in vain at the end of that time for the promised *Nunc dimittis*. He has now found a new sphere of activity. Hitherto his duties have precluded him from more than an occasional attendance at the Cathedral services. Now he begins to take an interest in the fabric and the music. Upon his struggles with the organist, an old gentleman who had been in office since 1786, I have no time to dwell; they were not attended with any marked success. More to the purpose is his sudden growth of enthusiasm for the Cathedral itself and its furniture. There is a draft of a letter to Sylvanus Urban (which I do not think was ever sent) describing the stalls in the choir. As I have said, these were of fairly late date – of about the year 1700, in fact.

'The archdeacon's stall, situated at the south-east end, west of the episcopal throne (now so worthily occupied by the truly excellent prelate who adorns the See of Barchester), is distinguished by some curious ornamentation. In addition to the arms of Dean West, by whose efforts the whole of the internal furniture of the choir was completed, the prayer-desk is terminated at the eastern extremity by three small but remarkable statuettes in the grotesque manner. One is an exquisitely modelled figure of a cat, whose crouching posture suggests with admirable spirit the suppleness, vigilance, and craft of the redoubted adversary of the genus *Mus*. Opposite to this is a figure seated upon a throne and invested with the attributes of royalty; but it is no earthly monarch whom the carver has sought to portray. His feet are studiously concealed by the long robe in which he is draped: but neither the crown nor the cap which he wears suffice to hide the prick-ears and curving horns which betray his Tartarean origin; and the hand which rests upon his knee is armed with talons of horrifying length and sharpness. Between these two figures stands a shape muffled in a long mantle. This might at first sight be mistaken for a monk or "friar of orders grey", for the head is cowled and a knotted cord depends from somewhere about the waist. A slight inspection, however, will lead to a very different conclusion. The knotted cord is quickly seen to be a halter, held by a hand all but concealed within the draperies; while the sunken features and, horrid to relate, the rent flesh upon the cheek-bones, proclaim the King of Terrors. These figures are evidently the production of no unskilled chisel; and should it chance that any of your correspondents are able to throw light upon their origin and significance, my obligations to your valuable miscellany will be largely increased.'

There is more description in the paper, and, seeing that the woodwork in question has now disappeared, it has a considerable interest. A paragraph at the end is worth quoting:

'Some late researches among the Chapter accounts have shown me that the carving of the stalls was not, as was very usually reported, the work of Dutch artists, but was executed by a native of this city or district named Austin. The timber was procured from an oak copse in the vicinity, the property of the Dean and Chapter, known as Holywood. Upon a recent visit to the parish within whose boundaries it is situated, I learned from the aged and truly respectable incumbent that traditions still lingered amongst the inhabitants of the great size and age of the oaks employed to furnish the materials of the stately structure which has been, however imperfectly, described in the above lines. Of one in particular, which stood near the centre of the grove, it is remembered that it was known as the Hanging Oak. The propriety of that title is confirmed by the fact that a quantity of human bones was found in the soil about its roots, and that at certain times of the year it was the custom for those who wished to secure a successful issue to their affairs, whether of love or the ordinary business of life, to suspend from its boughs small images or puppets rudely fashioned of straw, twigs, or the like rustic materials.'

So much for the archdeacon's archaeological investigations. To return to his career as it is to be gathered from his diaries. Those of his first three years of hard and careful work show him throughout in high spirits, and, doubtless, during this time, that reputation for hospitality and urbanity which is mentioned in his obituary notice was well deserved. After that, as time goes on, I see a shadow coming over him – destined to develop into utter blackness – which I cannot but think must have been reflected in his outward demeanour. He commits a good deal of his fears and troubles to his diary; there was no other outlet for them. He was unmarried, and his sister was not always with him. But I am much mistaken if he has told all that he might have told. A series of extracts shall be given:

Aug. 30, 1816 – The days begin to draw in more perceptibly than ever. Now that the Archdeaconry papers are reduced to order, I must find some further employment for the evening hours of autumn and winter. It is a great blow that Letitia's health will not allow her to stay through these months. Why not go on with my *Defence of Episcopacy*? It may be useful.

Sept. 15 – Letitia has left me for Brighton.

Oct. 11 – Candles lit in the choir for the first time at evening prayers. It came as a shock: I find that I absolutely shrink from the dark season.

Nov. 17 – Much struck by the character of the carving on my desk: I do not know that I had ever carefully noticed it before. My attention was called to it by an accident. During the *Magnificat* I was, I regret to say, almost overcome with sleep. My hand was resting on the back of the carved figure of a cat which is the nearest to me of the three figures on the end of my stall. I was not aware of this, for I was not looking in that direction, until I was startled by what seemed a softness, a feeling as of rather rough and coarse fur, and a sudden movement, as if the creature were twisting round its head to bite me. I regained complete consciousness in an instant, and I have some idea that I must have uttered a suppressed exclamation, for I noticed that Mr Treasurer turned his head quickly in my direction. The impression of the unpleasant feeling was so strong that I found myself rubbing my hand upon my surplice. This accident led me to examine the figures after prayers more carefully than I had done before, and I realized for the first time with what skill they are executed.

Dec. 6 – I do indeed miss Letitia's company. The evenings, after I have worked as long as I can at my *Defence*, are very trying. The house is too large for a lonely man, and visitors of any kind are too rare. I get an uncomfortable impression when going to my room that there *is* company of some kind. The fact is (I may as well formulate it to myself) that I hear voices. This, I am well aware, is a common symptom of incipient decay of the brain – and I believe that I should be less disquieted than I am if I had any suspicion that this was the cause. I have none – none whatever, nor is there anything in my family history to give colour to such an idea. Work, diligent work, and a punctual attention to the duties which fall to me is my best remedy, and I have little doubt that it will prove efficacious.

Jan. 1 – My trouble is, I must confess it, increasing upon me. Last night, upon my return after midnight from the Deanery, I lit my candle to go upstairs. I was nearly at the top when something whispered to me, 'Let me wish you a happy New Year.' I could not be mistaken: it spoke distinctly and with a peculiar emphasis. Had I dropped my candle, as I all but did, I tremble to think what the consequences must have been. As it was, I managed to get up the last flight, and was quickly in my room with the door locked, and experienced no other disturbance.

Jan. 15 – I had occasion to come downstairs last night to my workroom for my watch, which I had inadvertently left on my table when I went up to bed. I think I was at the top of the last flight when I had a sudden impression of a sharp whisper in my ear *'Take care.'* I clutched the balusters and naturally looked round at once. Of course, there was nothing. After a moment I went on – it was no good turning back – but I had as nearly as possible fallen: a cat – a large one by the feel of it – slipped between my feet, but again, of course, I saw nothing. It *may* have been the kitchen cat, but I do not think it was.

Feb. 27 – A curious thing last night, which I should like to forget. Perhaps if I put it down here I may see it in its true proportion. I worked in the library from about 9 to 10. The hall and staircase seemed to be unusually full of what I can only call movement without sound: by this I mean that there seemed to be continuous going and coming, and that whenever I ceased writing to listen, or looked out into the hall, the stillness was absolutely unbroken. Nor, in going to my room at an earlier hour than usual – about half-past ten – was I conscious of anything that I could call a noise. It so happened that I had told John to come to my room for the letter to the bishop which I wished to have delivered early in the morning at the Palace. He was to sit up, therefore, and come for it when he heard me retire. This I had for the moment forgotten, though I had remembered to carry the letter with me to my room. But when, as I was winding up my watch, I heard a light tap at the door,

and a low voice saying, 'May I come in?' (which I most
undoubtedly did hear), I recollected the fact, and took
up the letter from my dressing-table, saying, 'Certainly:
come in.' No one, however, answered my summons,
and it was now that, as I strongly suspect, I committed
an error: for I opened the door and held the letter out.
There was certainly no one at that moment in the passage, but, in the instant of my standing there, the door
at the end opened and John appeared carrying a candle.
I asked him whether he had come to the door earlier;
but am satisfied that he had not. I do not like the situation; but although my senses were very much on the
alert, and though it was some time before I could sleep,
I must allow that I perceived nothing further of an unto-
ward character.

With the return of spring, when his sister came to live
with him for some months, Dr Haynes's entries become
more cheerful, and, indeed, no symptom of depression
is discernible until the early part of September, when he
was again left alone. And now, indeed, there is evidence
that he was incommoded again, and that more press-
ingly. To this matter I will return in a moment, but I
digress to put in a document which, rightly or wrongly,
I believe to have a bearing on the thread of the story.

The account-books of Dr Haynes, preserved along

with his other papers, show, from a date but little later than that of his institution as archdeacon, a quarterly payment of 25 to J. L. Nothing could have been made of this, had it stood by itself. But I connect with it a very dirty and ill-written letter, which, like another that I have quoted, was in a pocket in the cover of a diary. Of date or postmark there is no vestige, and the decipherment was not easy. It appears to run:

Dr Sr

I have bin expctin to her off you theis last wicks, and not Haveing done so must supose you have not got mine witch was saying how me and my man had met in with bad times this season all seems to go cross with us on the farm and which way to look for the rent we have no knowledge of it this been the sad case with us if you would have the great [liberality *probably, but the exact spelling defies reproduction*] to send fourty pounds otherwise steps will have to be took which I should not wish. Has you was the Means of me losing my place with Dr Pulteney I think it is only just what I am asking and you know best what I could say if I was Put to it but I do not wish anything of that unpleasant Nature being one that always wish to have everything Pleasant about me.

Your obedt Servt, Jane Lee

About the time at which I suppose this letter to have been written there is, in fact, a payment of £40 to J. L.

We return to the diary:

Oct. 22 – At evening prayers, during the Psalms, I had that same experience which I recollect from last year. I was resting my hand on one of the carved figures, as before (I usually avoid that of the cat now), and – I was going to have said – a change came over it, but that seems attributing too much importance to what must, after all, be due to some physical affection in myself: at any rate, the wood seemed to become chilly and soft as if made of wet linen. I can assign the moment at which I became sensible of this. The choir were singing the words *(Set thou an ungodly man to be ruler over him and) let Satan stand at his right hand.*

The whispering in my house was more persistent tonight. I seemed not to be rid of it in my room. I have not noticed this before. A nervous man, which I am not, and hope I am not becoming, would have been much annoyed, if not alarmed, by it. The cat was on the stairs tonight. I think it sits there always. There *is* no kitchen cat.

Nov. 15 – Here again I must note a matter I do not understand. I am much troubled in sleep. No definite image presented itself, but I was pursued by the very vivid impression that wet lips were whispering into my ear with great rapidity and emphasis for some time together. After this, I suppose, I fell asleep, but was awakened with a start by a feeling as if a hand were laid on my shoulder. To my intense alarm I found myself standing at the top of the lowest flight of the first staircase. The moon was shining brightly enough through the large window to let me see that there was a large cat on the second or third step. I can make no comment. I crept up to bed again, I do not know how. Yes, mine is a heavy burden. [Then follows a line or two which has been scratched out. I fancy I read something like 'acted for the best'.]

Not long after this it is evident to me that the archdeacon's firmness began to give way under the pressure of these phenomena. I omit as unnecessarily painful and distressing the ejaculations and prayers which, in the months of December and January, appear for the first time and become increasingly frequent. Throughout this time, however, he is obstinate in clinging to his post. Why he did not plead ill-health and take refuge at Bath or Brighton I cannot tell; my impression is that it would have done him no good; that he was a man who, if he had confessed himself beaten by the annoyances, would have succumbed at once, and that he was conscious of this. He did seek to palliate them by inviting visitors to his house. The result he has noted in this fashion:

Jan. 7 – I have prevailed on my cousin Allen to give me a few days, and he is to occupy the chamber next to mine.

Jan. 8 – A still night. Allen slept well, but complained of the wind. My own experiences were as before: still whispering and whispering: what is it that he wants to say?

Jan. 9 – Allen thinks this a very noisy house. He thinks, too, that my cat is an unusually large and fine specimen, but very wild.

Jan. 10 – Allen and I in the library until 11. He left me twice to see what the maids were doing in the hall: returning the second time he told me he had seen one of them passing through the door at the end of the passage, and said if his wife were here she would soon get them into better order. I asked him what coloured dress the maid wore; he said grey or white. I supposed it would be so.

Jan. 11 – Allen left me today. I must be firm.

These words, *I must be firm*, occur again and again on subsequent days; sometimes they are the only entry. In these cases they are in an unusually large hand, and dug into the paper in a way which must have broken the pen that wrote them.

Apparently the archdeacon's friends did not remark any change in his behaviour, and this gives me a high idea of his courage and determination. The diary tells us nothing more than I have indicated of the last days of his life. The end of it all must be told in the polished language of the obituary notice:

The morning of the 26th of February was cold and tempestuous. At an early hour the servants had occasion to go into the front hall of the residence occupied by the lamented subject of these lines. What was their horror upon observing the form of their beloved and respected master lying upon the landing of the principal staircase in an attitude which inspired the gravest fears. Assistance was procured, and an universal consternation was experienced upon the discovery that he had been the object of a brutal and a murderous attack. The vertebral column was fractured in more than one place. This might have been the result of a fall: it appeared that the stair-carpet was loosened at one point. But, in addition to this, there were injuries inflicted upon the eyes, nose and mouth, as if by the agency of some savage animal, which, dreadful to relate, rendered those features unrecognizable. The vital spark was, it is needless to add, completely extinct, and had been so, upon the testimony of respectable medical authorities, for several hours. The author or authors of this mysterious outrage are alike buried in mystery, and the most active

conjecture has hitherto failed to suggest a solution of
the melancholy problem afforded by this appalling
occurrence.

The writer goes on to reflect upon the probability that
the writings of Mr Shelley, Lord Byron, and M. Voltaire
may have been instrumental in bringing about the disaster, and concludes by hoping, somewhat vaguely, that
this event may 'operate as an example to the rising generation'; but this portion of his remarks need not be
quoted in full.

I had already formed the conclusion that Dr Haynes
was responsible for the death of Dr Pulteney. But the
incident connected with the carved figure of death
upon the archdeacon's stall was a very perplexing fea-
ture. The conjecture that it had been cut out of the
wood of the Hanging Oak was not difficult, but seemed
impossible to substantiate. However, I paid a visit to
Barchester, partly with the view of finding out whether
there were any relics of the woodwork to be heard of. I
was introduced by one of the canons to the curator of
the local museum, who was, my friend said, more likely
to be able to give me information on the point than anyone else. I told this gentleman of the description of
certain carved figures and arms formerly on the stalls,
and asked whether any had survived. He was able to

show me the arms of Dean West and some other frag-
ments. These, he said, had been got from an old resident,
who had also once owned a figure – perhaps one of
those which I was inquiring for. There was a very odd
thing about that figure, he said. 'The old man who had
it told me that he picked it up in a woodyard, whence
he had obtained the still extant pieces, and had taken it
home for his children. On the way home he was fid-
dling about with it and it came in two in his hands, and
a bit of paper dropped out. This he picked up and, just
noticing that there was writing on it, put it into his
pocket, and subsequently into a vase on his mantel-
piece. I was at his house not very long ago, and happened
to pick up the vase and turn it over to see whether there
were any marks on it, and the paper fell into my hand.
The old man, on my handing it to him, told me the
story I have told you, and said I might keep the paper. It
was crumpled and rather torn, so I have mounted it on
a card, which I have here. If you can tell me what it
means I shall be very glad, and also, I may say, a good
deal surprised.'

He gave me the card. The paper was quite legibly
inscribed in an old hand, and this is what was on it:

When I grew in the Wood
I was water'd wth Blood

Now in the Church I stand
Who that touches me with his Hand
If a Bloody hand he bear
I councell him to be ware
Lest he be fetcht away
Whether by night or day,
But chiefly when the wind blows high
In a night of February.
This I drempt, 26 Febr. A° 1699. JOHN AUSTIN.

'I suppose it is a charm or a spell: wouldn't you call it something of that kind?' said the curator.

'Yes,' I said, 'I suppose one might. What became of the figure in which it was concealed?'

'Oh, I forgot,' said he. 'The old man told me it was so ugly and frightened his children so much that he burnt it.'

RYŪNOSUKE AKUTAGAWA *Hell Screen*

KINGSLEY AMIS *Dear Illusion*

SAUL BELLOW *Him With His Foot in His Mouth*

DONALD BARTHELME *Some of Us Had Been Threatening Our Friend Colby*

SAMUEL BECKETT *The Expelled*

JORGE LUIS BORGES *The Widow Ching – Pirate*

PAUL BOWLES *The Delicate Prey*

ITALO CALVINO *The Queen's Necklace*

ALBERT CAMUS *The Adulterous Woman*

TRUMAN CAPOTE *Children on Their Birthdays*

ANGELA CARTER *Bluebeard*

RAYMOND CHANDLER *Killer in the Rain*

EILEEN CHANG *Red Rose, White Rose*

G. K. CHESTERTON *The Strange Crime of John Boulnois*

JOSEPH CONRAD *Youth*

ROBERT COOVER *Romance of the Thin Man and the Fat Lady*

ISAK DINESEN *Babette's Feast*

MARGARET DRABBLE *The Gifts of War*

HANS FALLADA *Short Treatise on the Joys of Morphinism*

F. SCOTT FITZGERALD *Babylon Revisited*

IAN FLEMING *The Living Daylights*

E. M. FORSTER *The Machine Stops*

SHIRLEY JACKSON *The Tooth*

HENRY JAMES *The Beast in the Jungle*

a little history

Penguin Modern Classics were launched in 1961, and have been shaping the reading habits of generations ever since.

The list began with distinctive grey spines and evocative pictorial covers – a look that, after various incarnations, continues to influence their current design – and with books that are still considered landmark classics today.

Penguin Modern Classics have caused scandal and political change, inspired great films and broken down barriers, whether social, sexual or the boundaries of language itself. They remain the most provocative, groundbreaking, exciting and revolutionary works of the last 100 years (or so).

In 2011, on the fiftieth anniversary of the Modern Classics, we're publishing fifty Mini Modern Classics: the very best short fiction by writers ranging from Beckett to Conrad, Nabokov to Saki, Updike to Wodehouse. Though they don't take long to read, they'll stay with you long after you turn the final page.

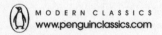

MODERN CLASSICS
www.penguinclassics.com